P9-BZE-838

STAR WARS
Search Your Feelings

GALACTIC BASIC EDITION

WRITTEN BY CALLIOPE GLASS & CAITLIN KENNEDY
ILLUSTRATED BY KATIE COOK

Los Angeles • New York

Printed in the United States of America

First Edition, October 2018 10 9 8 7 6 5 4 3 2 1

Library of Congress Control Number on file

FAC-038091-18236

ISBN 978-1-368-02736-6

Designed by Leigh Zieske

Visit the official *Star Wars* website at: www.starwars.com.

Logo Applies to Text Stock Only

An adventure in
rhyme and space awaits.
Search your feelings.
You know it to be true....

EXCITED

Long before he turned
To the dark side, oh so scary,
Little Anakin, just a boy,
Was quite the contrary.

He wanted to fight for what was right,
So he gave Qui-Gon the slip.
And with R2 he flew into space
And blew up a battleship.

Anakin was **excited**, elated, ecstatic.
He knew he had saved the day.
He would begin Jedi training
And learn from the best.
He wanted to start right away!

JEALOUS

Anakin Skywalker is strong in the Force
And a very powerful Jedi.
He wants a promotion
To Master, of course,
Which the Council is quick to deny.

Anakin Skywalker is stuck as a Knight,
And the rejection hurts his pride.
He's **jealous**, resentful, and bitter, you see.
He's heading toward the dark side.

EMBARRASSED

Jar Jar's a hungry Gungan.
His belly never stops rumblin'.
So when he spied a snack,
He opened his trap
And tried to gobble it, fumblin'.

See, Qui-Gon's a Jedi Master.
His reflexes work a bit faster.
He grabbed Jar Jar's tongue,
Leaving him **embarrassed**. No fun!
This dinner had turned to disaster.

AFRAID

Padmé has a secret,
One she's **afraid** to tell.
Worried and frightened,
She waits and she frets.
Her concerns she can't dispel.

She married her friend Anakin,
And now they're having twins.
The problem is their love is forbidden.
And thus all their trouble begins.

© LFL

SUSPICIOUS

Sinister Sidious,
Chancellor Palpatine–
Two who were really one.
A Sith Lord
With an evil plan.
Though who suspected, none?

Not quite so.
There was one person
Who was a bit **suspicious**.
Mace Windu,
In all his wisdom,
Sensed Palpatine was vicious.

HOPEFUL

One bright star
Is how it all began.
The Rebellion. The Resistance.
The princess with the plan.

Leia understood.
She knew the Empire's demands.
Her ship was under attack.
She held the future in her hands.

Hopeful, she hurried
And hid her treasure well.
All because of Leia,
We have the greatest tale to tell.

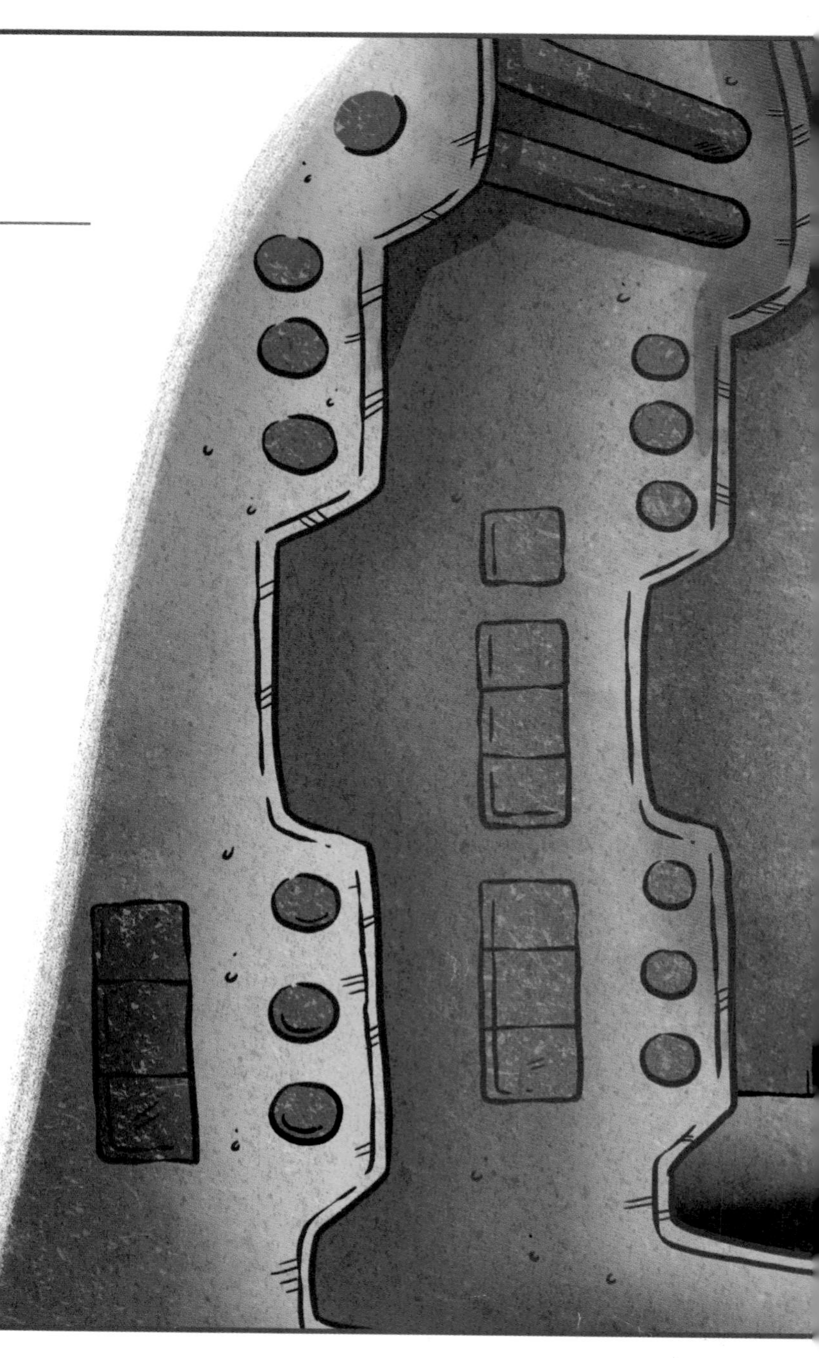

CONFUSED

“These aren’t the droids you’re looking for,”
The old man calmly stated.
But the stormtroopers were **confused**,
Mixed-up, and agitated.

For these *were* the droids the troopers needed.
Surely, the old man was wrong.
But Obi-Wan just waved his hand.
And the troopers said, “Move along.”

CONFIDENT

A secret mission, an important task.
Obi-Wan needed a ride, no questions asked.
Han offered his service,
Confident, not nervous.
After all, the *Falcon* was fast.

DISGUSTED

Stinky, smelly, rotten, putrid,
A trash compactor is no fun.
Then again, say what you will,
They're not bad if you're on the run.

But something's moving underfoot,
And the walls are closing in.
Maybe compactors aren't so great
When you're trying to save your skin.

Leia, Luke, Han, and Chewie,
Disgusted and stuck in slime,
Frantically call Threepio
To get out just in time.

CALM

Calm and steady,
Strong and still,
Reaching out
With pure will.

Yoda stands,
A Master Jedi,
Cane in hand,
Head held high.

He feels the Force–
Flowing, flexing–
And raises up...
A dripping X-wing.

GUILTY

Han had counted on Lando, his buddy,
To hide him from the Empire.
Lando's loyalties may have been a bit muddy,
But against Han he would never conspire!

Poor Han had been wrong.
He couldn't believe it.
He'd been as wrong as one could be.

Lando was **guilty**.
And Vader was there.
And Han had no way to flee.

SURPRISED

Luke thought he was an orphan,
The only Skywalker around.
But the boy was in for quite a shock.
The truth would truly astound.

The mysterious villain,
The evil Darth Vader,
Was actually a Skywalker–
A Jedi named Anakin, a hero who'd turned,
And most shocking of all, Luke's father!

Poor young Luke was startled and stunned.
He was just so very **surprised**.
He wasn't a baby; he was almost grown.
But he couldn't help it ... so he cried.

ANXIOUS

A protocol droid in a chair,
As **anxious** as could be.
He rose from the ground
And spun through the air
And shrieked like a banshee.

The Ewoks were very impressed.
They thought Threepio was a god.
But it was really Luke using the Force
As the Ewoks oohed and aahed.

SAD

A droid is made up
Of many a part,
But if you didn't know it,
You'd think Artoo had a heart!

Luke's faithful friend,
The droid long served him well.
But when the Jedi disappeared,
Into despair Artoo fell!

For years the droid sat.
He sulked and he pined,
Feeling **sad** and blue.
Artoo had been left behind.

Where was his master?
Would he see him again?
Artoo waited and wondered
And longed for his friend.

DETERMINED

Rey didn't think. She acted.
And the Force flowed freely through her.
Evil may have lain ahead.
But she was the hope for the future.

Rey was **determined**.
Rey was ready.
She knew what she had to do.
She raised her arm, reached out with the Force,
And to *her* the lightsaber flew.

LONELY

A Jedi Master
On an island,
Luke knows Ahch-To
From beach to highland.

He knows its caves,
Its craggy shores.
He wanders around
And does his chores.

He goes to the temple
And reads some old books.
He sits by himself,
And sometimes he cooks.

The sole human around,
The one and the only,
He thinks he's okay,
But I think he's **lonely**.

ANGRY

Kylo Ren has anger issues.
I think that's safe to say.
He smashed his own helmet
And ruined an elevator
And blew up a hangar bay.

Then again, his boss had called him a failure.
So can you blame him for being a bit mad?
Let's all agree that Snoke is the reason
Why Kylo's such an **angry** lad.

FRUSTRATED

This **frustrated** Wookiee's vexation
Has porgs as its chief aggravation.
They're so cute, it's cloying.
There's nothing more annoying
Than an adorable porg infestation.

DISTRACTED

ᴰᴵˢᵀᴿᴬᶜᵀᴱᴰ

In the glitzy heart of Canto Bight,
Shining, glittering, glaring, bright,
Finn is there on a secret mission,
But he quickly starts to raise suspicion.

He can't stay focused.
There's too much to see,
From the jewels to the gold.
He gasps audibly.

So **distracted** is the starry-eyed Finn,
Rose has to remind him why they snuck in!

HAPPY

A pilot and a droid.
Is there any bond quite so tight?
If Poe and BB-8 are apart,
Something just doesn't feel right.

These two are meant to be together.
Sure, that may sound sappy.
But that's why when they reunite,
They are both just so darn **happy**.

Was that the end of the book?

I have a bad feeling about this.
I thought that was *my* line....
Dear, oh dear...

EXCITED
JEALOUS
EMBARRASSED
AFRAID
SUSPICIOUS
HOPEFUL
CONFUSED
CONFIDENT
Search Your Feelings

DISGUSTED
CALM
GUILTY
SURPRISED
ANXIOUS
SAD
DETERMINED
LONELY
ANGRY
FRUSTRATED
DISTRACTED
HAPPY

CALLIOPE GLASS

Calliope Glass is a children's book writer and editor in New York City. Her favorite *Star Wars* character is Mon Mothma. She likes to solve crossword puzzles, read comic books, and sing very loudly.

CAITLIN KENNEDY

Caitlin Kennedy lives in San Francisco with her husband, mere miles from the redwoods that inspired the forests of Endor. She has yet to see an Ewok.

KATIE COOK

Katie Cook is an illustrator and writer who has been creating work for *Star Wars* professionally for almost a decade, and unprofessionally with crayons since the mid-1980s. She lives in Michigan with her husband, her daughters, and lots of *Star Wars* toys . . . er, collectibles.